THE BOY AND THE TIGER

AND OTHER STORIES FOR 9-11 YEAR OLDS

Other Stories in this series:

The Gingerbread Man *and other stories for 4 -7 year olds*

Dragonory *and other stories for 7-9 year olds*

Compiled by
PIE CORBETT

SCHOLASTIC

To all those parents, storytellers and teachers who keep the flame of stories alive in children's minds.

To Edmund - more stories for your golden box.

Designed using Adobe InDesign

Published by Scholastic Ltd
Book End
Range Road
Witney
Oxfordshire
OX29 0YD
www.scholastic.co.uk

Printed and bound by CPI Group (UK) Ltd, Croydon, CR0 4YY

6 7 8 9   4 5 6 7

British Library Cataloguing-in-Publication Data
A catalogue record for this book is available from the British Library.

ISBN 978-1407-10066-1

Acknowledgements

Every effort has been made to trace copyright holders for the works reproduced in this book, and the publishers apologise for any inadvertent omissions.

Pie Corbett for the use *The Man in Search of his Luck, The Impossible Escape, The Cobbler and the Dragon*, and *Cinderella* retold by Pie Corbett © 2008, Pie Corbett (2008, previously unpublished).

Jane Grell for the use of *Nyangara, the Fire Python* retold by Jane Grell © 2008, Jane Grell (2008, previously unpublished).

Xanthe Gresham and **Michael Harvey** for the use of *Pumpkin* retold by Xanthe Gresham and Michael Harvey © 2008, Xanthe Gresham and Michael Harvey (2008, previously unpublished).

Patricia Leighton for the use of *The Widow's Daughters* retold by Patricia Leighton © 2008, Patricia Leighton (2008, previously unpublished).

Hugh Lupton for the use of *Bella and the Bear* retold by Hugh Lupton from 'Early Years Activity Bank - April 2007' © 2007, Hugh Lupton (2007, Scholastic).

Daniel Morden for the use of *Six go Through the World* and *The Boy and the Tiger* both retold by Daniel Morden © 2008, Daniel Morden (2008, previously unpublished).

Brian Patten for the use of *Regrets* retold by Brian Patten © 2008, Brian Patten (2008, previously unpublished).

Andrew and Polly Fusek Peters for the use *Ragamuffin and his Delicious Nail Soup* retold by Andrew Fusek Peters © 2008, Andrew Fusek Peters (2008, previously unpublished)

Taffy Thomas for the use of *The Fearsome Giant* and *The Farmer's Fun-Loving Daughter* both retold by Taffy Thomas © 2008, Taffy Thomas (2008, previously unpublished).

Helen East for *Aldar Kose's Cloak* retold by Helen East © 2008, Helen East (2008, previously unpublished).

The publishers would like to thank Xanthe Gresham, Pie Corbett and Taffy Thomas for their readings on the audio CD and also Linden Studios and Adrian Moss for the audio CD development.

Contents

Introduction 7

1. **The Man in Search of his Luck**
Pie Corbett..9
2. **Six Go Through the World**
Daniel Morden 18
3. **Pumpkin**
Xanthe Gresham.. 30
4. **The Boy and the Tiger**
Daniel Morden 42
5. **Aldar-Kose's Cloak**
Helen East.. 48
6. **The Fearsome Giant**
Taffy Thomas 54
7. **Nyangara, the Fire Python**
Jane Grell 65
8. **Regrets**
Brian Patten 75

Contents continued

9. **The Impossible Escape**
Pie Corbett 79

10. **The Widow's Daughters**
Patricia Leighton 83

11. **The Cobbler and the Dragon**
Pie Corbett 93

12. **Ragamuffin and his Delicious Nail Soup**
Andrew Fusek Peters 99

13. **The Farmer's Fun-Loving Daughter**
Taffy Thomas 107

14. **Bella and the Bear**
Hugh Lupton 115

15. **Cinderella**
Pie Corbett 131

Author biographies 140

Introduction

Three golden apples fall from heaven –
one is for the person who tells the tale;
one is for the person who listens;
and one is for the person who passes it on.

Storytelling weaves a spell that binds us all into one world community. We enter that other world where anything is possible and we can think, feel and grow together. Stories help sustain and create our community. They help to fashion who we are and to know what is right and what is wrong. Stories cherish the human spirit within ourselves and within the children who listen to and tell them.

All cultures have songs, art, dance, religion – and of course, stories. Without the stories of our culture, we have no culture.

Research has shown that children who are read to and hear stories before going to school are the most likely to succeed in school. This is because stories help children to sit still, listen and concentrate; they also help to develop abstract thinking so that children who have had stories told or read to them are the first to form abstract concepts across the curriculum. In addition, stories create a comforting imaginative world in which ogres can be confronted and our deepest fears played out and controlled.

It is worth noticing how the most proficient writers in any class are readers. They are children who were probably read to before they went to school, have a bedtime story every night and have become avid readers themselves. This constant repetition of listening to and reading stories has helped them internalise the patterns they need to create stories of their own. Because you cannot create stories out of nothing.

Pie Corbett 2008

The Man in Search of his Luck

Retold by Pie Corbett

Once there was a man upon whom luck had never smiled. Why, his friends had deceived him, his sons had robbed him and he found himself without friends, family or fortune.

One day he heard that the Undying Sun had brought wealth to the penniless and luck to the unfortunate. So he decided to travel to the end of the world where some said the Undying Sun might be found.

So he walked and he walked and he walked, 'til he came to a rocky valley where there was a lion – a lean lion, a mean lion, with fierce red eyes and sharp white teeth.

"I'm travelling to the end of the earth to find the Undying Sun and to ask where I might find some luck," said the man to the lion.

"If you find the Undying Sun, will you ask two questions for me?" growled the lion.

"Of course," said the man.

"Very well, ask why I am so thin and what can be done about that."

So the man set off again, and he walked and he walked and he walked until he came to a lake where a fish floated on the shimmering surface.

"I'm travelling to the end of the earth to find the Undying Sun and to ask where I might find some luck," said the man to the fish.

"If you find someone who can help, will you ask two questions for me?" asked the fish.

"Of course," replied the man.

"Very well, ask why I cannot swim in the cool waters below and what can be done about that."

So the man set off again, and he walked and he walked and he walked until he came to a place where an oak tree spread its branches, but the leaves were dropping and dying even though it was summer.

"I'm travelling to the end of the earth to find the Undying Sun and to ask where I might find some luck," said the man to the tree.

"If you find someone who can help, will you ask two questions for me?" asked the tree in a voice as rich as the earth itself.

"Of course," replied the man.

"Very well, ask why my leaves are dying and what can be done about that."

So, the man set off again and he walked and he walked and he walked until he came to a place where a girl was crying bitterly.

"I'm travelling to the end of the earth to find the Undying Sun and to ask where I might find some luck," said the man to the girl.

"If you find someone who can help, will you ask two questions for me?" sobbed the girl.

"Of course," replied the man.

"Very well, ask why I am so sad and what can be done about that."

So, the man set off again and he walked and he walked and he walked until he came to the very edge of the earth. Clouds billowed, rain drifted and buzzards swooped. There he met the Undying Sun.

"Pray tell me, why am I so unlucky and what can be done about it?" the unlucky man asked.

"There is plenty of luck for you and it is just waiting," chortled the Undying Sun. "You will find it right under your nose."

So, sooner rather than later, the unlucky man had answers to not one, not two, not three but four sets of questions. Excited by the prospect of his good fortune, he ran and he ran and he ran. Soon he came to the place where the girl was crying.

"I've been promised some luck. It'll be right under my nose and I'm on my way to find it!" he shouted.

"I'm pleased for you," sniffed the girl. "But

what about me? Why am I so sad?"

"That's easy! You are sad because you are lonely," replied the unlucky man.

"Well, what can be done about it?" sniffed the girl.

"That's easy! You must marry the first handsome young man who passes by and the pair of you will live happily ever after."

There was a short pause.

"Will you marry me then?" asked the girl, staring at him intently.

"Oh, sorry, but I'm on my way to find my luck!" shouted the unlucky man.

So, he ran and he ran and he ran. Soon he came to the place where the oak tree was waiting as patient as time itself.

"I've been promised some luck. It'll be right under my nose and I'm on my way to find it!" he shouted.

"I'm pleased for you," grumbled the tree. "But what about me? Why are my leaves dying?"

"That's easy! They are dying because your roots are blocked by a marbled chest containing gold and can no longer suck up enough water," replied the unlucky man.

"What can be done about it?" grumbled the tree hopefully.

"That's easy! You must stop the first strong young man who passes by and ask him to dig up the treasure chest and take it away."

There was a short pause.

"You look strong. Will you dig up the chest and take it away?" the tree asked, staring at him intently.

"Sorry, I'm on my way to find my luck!" shouted the unlucky man.

So he ran and he ran and he ran. Soon he came to the place where the fish still swam on the hot surface of the lake.

"I've been promised some luck. It'll be right under my nose and I'm on my way to find it!" he shouted.

"I'm pleased for you," hissed the fish. "But what about me? Why can I only swim on the surface?"

"That's easy! You have a blister on your head that must be burst," replied the unlucky man.

"What can be done about it?" hissed the fish.

"That's easy! You must asked someone carrying a stick to break it open."

There was a short pause.

"Would you do that for me?" the fish asked, staring at him intently.

"Very well," said the man, raising his staff and tapping the fish on its head.

As the blister broke, a large diamond tumbled on to the bank.

"I have no use for diamonds," said the fish as it plunged down. "Take it as your reward."

But already the unlucky man was on his way.

So, he ran and he ran and he ran. Soon he came to the place where the lion was waiting, looking leaner than ever, looking meaner than ever. Why, you could see its ribs poking through its skin!

"Great news! I've been promised some luck. It'll be right under my nose and I'm on my way to find it," he shouted.

"I'm pleased for you," growled the lion.

"But what about me? Why am I so thin?"

Eyeing the man, the lion pawed the ground.

"Well, that's easy! You are thin because you are starving," replied the unlucky man.

"And what can be done about that?" growled the lion, staring at him intently.

"Oh, that's easy! You must stop the first fool that passes by and eat him up."

And so ... he did.

Six Go Through the World

Retold by Daniel Morden

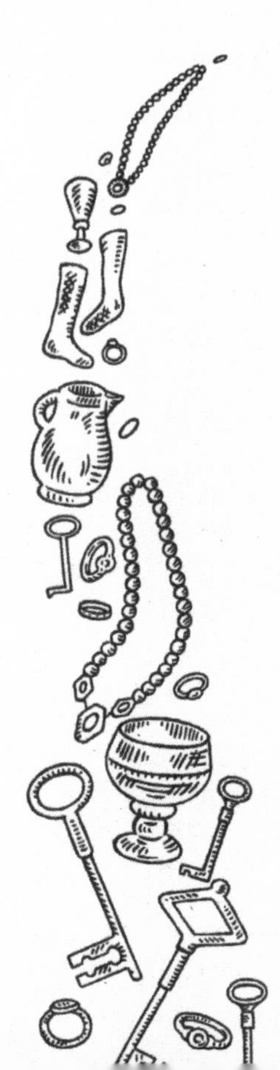

Once upon a time there was a war. Amongst the soldiers in the King's army there was a thief. He was a miraculous thief. He could steal the socks from your feet as you passed him in the street.

He was much in demand while the war was on, creeping into the enemy camp and stealing their plans, but as the war went on he became an irritation to the King.

He kept stealing food from the King's kitchen, stealing rings from the Queen's fingers to barter for wine.

Eventually the war ended. The thief was no longer useful, so the King slung him in prison. But the thief stole the keys and unlocked the door to his dungeon.

As he walked along the road, he passed a man with two sets of knees.

"Who are you? Tell me of yourself."

"I am the fastest runner in the world."

"I could do with one such as you. Come with us and we'll make our fortune."

Off they went together.

As the two of them walked, they came upon a man. One side of his face was like your face or my face, but the other side was one enormous eye. He lifted a rifle to his big eye and fired.

"What did you shoot?" said the thief.

"Three hundred miles away there's a wood. In the wood there's a tree. On the tree there's a branch. On the branch there's a fly. I just shot out the fly's left eye."

"I could do with one such as you. Come with us and we'll make our fortune."

Off they went together.

As the three of them walked they came upon a white man. His lips were white. His tongue was white. His hair was white. His face was covered in a fur of frost. His knees were

knocking, and his teeth were chattering. Mist was rising from his lips and his nostrils. He wore a hat at a jaunty angle.

The thief said, "Tell us of yourself."

"I wear this hat for a reason. If I straighten it, you know what happens? The world freezes, I mean rigid – birds fall from the sky, smashing into ponds."

"I could do with one such as you. Come with us and we'll make our fortune."

Off they went together.

As they travelled, they came upon a burly man bearing six trees on his shoulder as if they were stalks of corn.

The thief said, "Tell us of yourself."

"I am the strongest man in the world."

"I could do with one such as you. Come with us and we'll make our fortune."

"Maybe I will. But first of all I'll drop off this kindling for my mother."

Off they went together.

As they travelled, they came upon a man who was blowing. His cheeks bulged like balloons.

"What are you doing?"

"I'm turning the sails of a windmill three miles away."

"I could do with one such as you. Come with us and we'll make our fortune."

Off they went together.

They came to a village. Nailed to a tree was a sign which proclaimed if any man could outrun the Princess he could marry her.

"This is the way we'll make our fortune!" Off they went to the castle. You can imagine how pleased the King was to see the thief again. He smiled with his mouth but not with his eyes.

"You want to race my daughter?"

The thief bowed low. "Your Highness, my companion will run on my behalf."

"At the end of the world there is a well. The first runner to reach the well, scoop a glass of water and return with it is the winner. If your man wins, there'll be a wedding. If he loses, a beheading..."

The King pointed. On the battlements of the castle there were spikes. On each spike a human head. On each head stood a crow, pecking at an eye.

The two runners prepared themselves, and *whoosh!* off they went.

The runner streaked ahead. Within

moments he was so swift, he was invisible. The only sign that he'd passed by was a waft of wind stirring beards and skirts.

He filled the glass with water and set off back … but halfway, he began to tire. His legs ached, his joints were sore.

"I'm so far ahead," he thought, "I can afford a little rest … but I mustn't fall asleep! I know, I'll lie my head against this horse's skull. It's so uncomfortable I'll not nod off."

But within seconds he was snoring. The Princess passed by and saw him. She laughed. She tipped the glass on to the ground.

That would have been the end of this story were it not for the marksman. With his huge eye he had seen the slumbering runner. He fired a single shot. The bullet knocked the skull out from under the runner's head. The runner awoke with a jerk and saw the empty glass…

"All that I have done before does not deserve to be called running!" He returned to the well and *whoosh!* as swift as thought, he ran to the castle of the King.

The King smiled with his mouth but not with his eyes.

"Oh good! Very good! Let's celebrate the wedding! A feast!"

He led them to a lavishly decorated room - tapestries on the walls, rugs on the floors. A feast was fetched up from the kitchen.

But once they were inside, the door was locked and bolted. There was no keyhole for the thief to pick. The thief peeled back the corner of the rug. The floor was made of iron. He lifted the tapestries. The walls were made of iron. They were in a giant oven.

Outside, the cook lit a fire under the floor. The King was going to bake them to death.

The floor began to glow.

The walls began to glow.

The ceiling began to glow.

The frostbringer grinned. He lifted the hat from his ear.

Suddenly the six were shuddering. The whole room was filled with bitter cold. There were gales of hail and snow and frost...

The King waited for a while, then had the door opened... There were the six, shivering and blowing into their hands.

What was this? The fire beneath the floor was raging!

The King sidled over and said to the thief, "You win. I'll give you as much gold as you can carry if you'll renounce the claim on my daughter."

The thief agreed at once and fetched the Strong Man. They brought him a sack of gold. He lifted it without effort.

"More!" Another sack was brought.

"More!"

Sack after sack after sack... He shouldered six sacks full of gold!

"More!"

"That," said the King, "is all my gold."

Off they went. Once they were out of earshot, the King ordered, "Guards! Set forth from the castle and kill them all!"

Off went the guards.

"Look!" said the marksman. They turned and looked... A host of guards was galloping after them.

The blower took a deep breath and *blew!* The guards were tumbling through the sky.

The King saw his guards sailing over his castle. "Let the six go. There is magic in them."

And so the thief and his companions lived happily ever after.

Pumpkin

Retold by Xanthe Gresham

There was once a little old lady who was very, very old because she had seen many years, and very, very skinny because she didn't have enough to eat.

But she did have two dogs. How she loved her two dogs. She used to wake up every morning and say, "Oh, Tyson! Oh, Honey! What would I do without you?"

One thing this little old lady loved was getting something through the post. One morning a letter came through the door and she was very, very excited.

"It's my daughter's handwriting! Let's see..." She tore open the envelope.

Dear Mum,
I'm getting married. Please come. There will be lots of food and lots of dancing.
Love from your daughter.
PS Sorry, no dogs.

"Oh dear, Tyson. Oh dear, Honey. Will you stay and look after the house?"

"*Woof!*" said Tyson.

"*Grrrr... Woof!*" said Honey.

"Good dogs!" said the little old lady, and off she went through the dark forest to her daughter's wedding.

But because she was very, very old and very, very skinny she went very, very slowly.

Suddenly, out of the forest like a flaming red arrow, came Mr Fox.

"Little old lady," he sniffed, shaking his

bristling tail and flaring his sniffing nostrils, "I'm going to eat you now!"

"Oh, please don't eat me now!" said the old lady, her voice quavering and her eyes popping.

"*Because I'm on my way to my daughter's wedding, where there'll be lots of food. And right now I'm very, very skinny, but on my way back I'll be very, very fat! Eat me on the way back?*"

"*Sniff, sniff!*" bristled Mr Fox. "All right, I'll eat you on the way back!" And off he shot into the forest like a whizz-bang rocket.

"Oh dear! That was close!" said the little old lady and off she went, not quite so slowly, until out of the forest like a burst of golden light came Mr Lion.

"*Rarrr!* I'm going to eat you now, little old lady!" he roared, showing his sharp teeth.

"Oh please don't eat me now!" said the little old lady, her knees shaking and her teeth chattering.

> "*Because I'm on my way to my daughter's wedding, and right now I'm very, very skinny, but on my way back I'll be very, very fat! Eat me on the way back?*"

"*GRRRRRR* All rrrright then!" said Mr Lion. "I'll eat you on the way back!" And off he slunk into the forest like a sulky lump of custard.

"Oh dear! Oh dear!" said the little old lady, and she went a little faster.

Suddenly, out of the dark forest, like an ambling line of brown, appeared Mrs Bear.

"I'm going to eat you now. I'm going to eat you now, little old lady!" growled Mrs Bear, scratching the air with her long, sharp claws.

"Oh please don't eat me now!" said the little old lady, her heart pounding and her blood fizzing.

> "*Because I'm on my way to my daughter's wedding, and right now I'm very, very skinny, but on my way back I'll be very, very fat! Eat me on the way back?*"

"OK," said Mrs Bear, and off she whiffled into the forest, like a woolly furball.

The little old lady went on her way. She did a happy skip when she heard the beat of the music, smelled the sweetness of the food and saw her daughter's house in the distance.

Once she was at the wedding, she jived and bopped and wriggled and rocked and then she said, "Excuse me, excuse me," as she squeezed past the guests. "Excuse me, excuse me," as she squeezed past the bride and groom. "I'm just going to get a bite. Oh that looks nice! I'll have one of those – *ooooooh delicious,* two of those – *oooooh yummy,* and maybe ten of those – *ooooooh, all mine!*"

She ate and she ate and she ate and she ate. She ate for one day, she ate for two days and after three days she was no longer very, very skinny. She was very, very fat.

"Oh, daughter!" she said. "I've had a lovely

time. But I probably won't see you again because on my way home I'll either be eaten by Mrs Bear or Mr Lion or Mr Fox. But don't you worry about me, dear. I've had a lovely life!"

"Oh, Mum!" said her daughter, and took her into the garden where there was a gigantic pumpkin.

She took a knife and she sliced the pumpkin three times – side, down, across – and made a door. Inside she put a chair. She put her mother on the chair, and a tray of sweets on her mother's lap.

And then:

"*A one! A two! A threeeeee – whack!*"

She gave the pumpkin an almighty slap and off it rolled down the road with the little old lady inside holding on to her chair and her sweets.

"*Wheeeee!*" she giggled, as she bounced up and down. "*Wheeeeee!*" she chuckled, as she flew round and round, until the paw of Mrs

Bear made the pumpkin come to a sharp stop.

Inside, the little old lady bit her lip and whispered, "Oh dear!"

Mrs Bear sniffed at the pumpkin. She walked round the pumpkin. She scratched at the pumpkin, tasted it and... "*Yuk!*" She spat it out. "Don't like pumpkin!"

"*A one! A two! A threeeeee – whack!*"

Off it went down the road with the little old lady inside.

"*Wheeeee!*" she cried until the claw of Mr Lion made the pumpkin come to a sharp stop.

The little old lady screwed up her face very, very tight.

"Oh dear!" she said.

Mr Lion sniffed, he walked, he scratched, he tasted and...

"*Yuk!*" he roared. "Don't like pumpkin!"

"*A one! A two! A threeeeee – whack!*"

Off it went down the road with the little

old lady inside. "*Wheeeee!*" she cried until the nose of Mr Fox made the pumpkin come to a sharp stop.

Mr Fox sniffed once, sniffed twice, smiled a slow Mr Fox smile and sneered, "Old lady, *get out of the pumpkin!*"

The little old lady stamped her foot and pulled a face.

"I don't want to be eaten!" she said crossly to herself.

But when she opened the door of the pumpkin she smiled a little-old-lady smile and said, "Mr Fox, could I just have one old lady little request? Could I sing a little song before you eat me?"

> "*My two doggies, can you hear me?*
> *The fox is going to eat me.*
> *You'd better come quick.*
> *My two doggies, can you hear me?*
> *I'm so frightened I'm going to be sick!*"

Up jumped Tyson, up jumped Honey and they came barking, they came wagging, they came howling and chased Mr Fox into the forest and he was never seen again.

Back by the fire in her little old house, the little old lady said, "Oh Tyson! Oh Honey! What would I do without you? Now, I've saved some sweets from my daughter's wedding. Sit! That's one for you, Tyson, that's one for you, Honey, and one for me. *Mmm.*"

And as far as I know, they're chewing still.

The Boy and the Tiger

Retold by Daniel Morden

There was a boy. One time he was walking in the forest. He heard a strange sound. He followed the sound to a clearing. In the clearing there was a hole. In the hole there was a tiger.

Tiger said, "Oh, my child, please help me." So the boy pushed a long branch into the hole. Tiger climbed up the branch, sprang out of the hole and on to the boy.

The boy said, "I just saved your life and now you want to eat me? Is that justice?"

"Justice?" said Tiger. "My child, you are young. You do not yet know the ways of people. But you will learn soon. People are wicked."

"That is not true," said the boy. "People are not wicked."

"No?" said Tiger. "Ask Fig Tree."

The boy turned to Fig Tree. "Fig Tree, I saved Tiger's life and now he wants to eat me. Is that justice?"

"Justice?" said Fig Tree. "You are so young. You do not know the ways of people. Look at how they treat me. People take my fruit and cut me down and burn me in the fire. Is that justice?"

"Are you learning?" said Tiger. "Ask Cow."

"Cow," said the boy, "I just saved Tiger's life and now he wants to eat me. Is that justice?"

"Justice?" said Cow. "You are so young. You do not know how wicked people are. Look at me. All my life I have to keep giving birth. People steal my milk and my children and when I am old they kill me and eat me. You call that justice?"

"You see?" said Tiger.

"I do," said the boy.

Just then, down a tree came Monkey.

"Monkey," said the boy, "I just saved Tiger's life and now he wants to eat me. Is that justice?"

"You, a little boy, saved Tiger's life?" said Monkey.

"How?"

"I was in a hole," said Tiger.

"But you can jump!"

"It was too deep."

"But you can climb."

"The sides were mud."

"But you are Tiger! Everyone is scared of you! I cannot imagine a hole so steep with sides so slippery that you could not escape from it."

Tiger was angry.

"This is the hole! You see how deep it is?"

"That little hole?"

"It's big!"

"It's a mouse's hole!"

"It's a tiger trap! I couldn't get out! Look!"

He jumped into the hole … and quick as a flash, Monkey pulled out the branch.

Tiger roared, but it was too late. He was trapped all over again. Monkey and the boy walked away.

"You must admit, I just saved your life," said Monkey.

"That's true," said the boy.

"How will you repay me?"

"Come with me to the village," said the boy.

When they came to the village the boy whistled and out came his dogs. They chased and chased Monkey, snapping at his heels, until he scampered up a tree.

"I saved your life," said Monkey, "and now you set your dogs on me. Is that justice?"

"Justice?" said the boy. "Don't you know? People are wicked!"

Aldar-Kose's Cloak

Retold by Helen East

Ah Aldar-Kose! What a lad! Empty belly, but always merry. Nothing in his pocket, but a head full of tricks. And always a story to share.

Only one day it was cold, and the wind it did blow so, and his horse was old, and it did go so slow, and his cloak was nothing but holes, and even Aldar-Kose was beginning to feel cross. Until all of a sudden, he saw a rich man in a fox-fur coat on a fine young horse.

Aldar-Kose sat up with a smile, loosened his cloak and raised his voice.

"*Vo-ri-ra, ri-ra*
Vo-ri-ra-ra,
Vo-ri-ra-ra-ra."

The rich man stopped and stared at him.

"Why on earth," he said, "do you sing? Your horse hardly goes, and your cloak is full of holes – surely you must be terribly cold?"

Aldar-Kose looked up in surprise. Then he licked his finger and held it up high.

"Yes," he said, "I believe you're right. There is a cold wind blowing and quite soon it will be snowing. But I don't notice it like you do, because I've got holes to let the wind go through. Seventy holes all specially cut, to let it in and let it out. You see, it blows so fast, it goes straight by – so even if it snows, I'm snug and dry."

He tapped his horse and ambled on.

"*Vo-ri-ra, ri-ra*
Vo..."

"Wait!" said the rich man. "Please. I've a long way to go, and I wasn't expecting snow. Will you sell your cloak to me?"

"But then I'll get cold," said Aldar-Kose.

"I'll give you my fox fur too."

"*Mmm*," said Aldar-Kose. "I don't know. Your coat lets cold in up the sleeves … and I can't hurry home because my horse is slow."

"Then I'll give you my horse."

Aldar-Kose stopped and thought for a while.

"Well…" he said, "since you've asked me three times, I don't want to say no. But I'm not a businessman, so … hey, horse for horse, cloak for coat – that's a fair sort of swap. But your money, for my no money – that's not. So we'll leave it at the two, if that will do for you?"

"Done!" said the rich man quick as you can, before the other could change his mind.

He made the exchange, and went on his way, thinking, "My lucky day! The man's a fool. I got what I want and kept my money too!"

And Aldar-Kose, with his warm fur coat, and his fine, fast horse? He was singing of course! And he'd got a new story, too!

"*Vo-ri-ra, ri-ra*
Vo-ri-ra-ra."

Aldar-Kose's Cloak

The Fearsome Giant

Retold by
Taffy Thomas

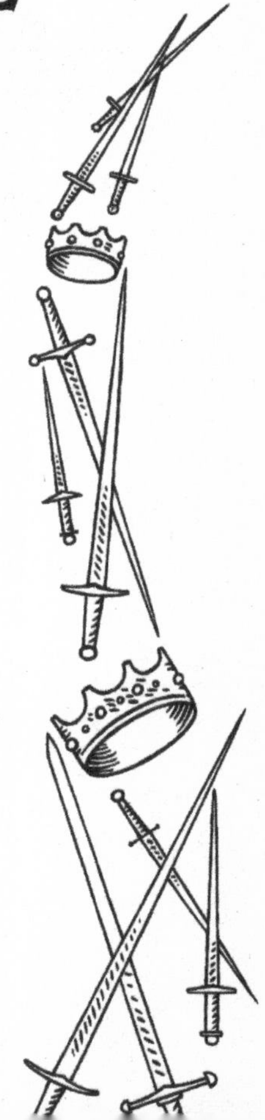

A long time ago, but not so long ago that no one can remember it, there was a land. And the land was a valley and running down the middle of the valley was a river and a road. But sadly the old King and Queen died. Now the day that the old King and Queen died, the crown passed to their son, the Prince. Now the Prince was very young – in fact, there were those that thought he was more child than man. And he was just a normal lad really, except for the fact that he was the Prince, and he wasn't particularly brave.

The day that he was crowned King, a fearsome giant moved into the valley. If anyone was travelling up the road by the river, the

giant would rear up in front of them and they would hear:

> "*SWISH! SWASH! BANG! BOOOM!*
> *I AMYOUR NIGHTMARE!*
> *I AMYOUR DOOM!*"

Followed by *splat!* as it trod on them.

All of the people went to the boy King and they said, "Your Highness, we're being terrorised by the fearsome giant. Something must be done to rid us of this giant."

And the boy King knew he had to do something about it, but he wasn't particularly brave, but he was the King. And because he was the King, he had soldiers and he thought he could get soldiers to do the dirty work, which is what kings and politicians have thought since time immemorial. So he picked his three bravest soldiers, the SAS of knights. And he said, "Right! You three, on your horses,

down the valley and destroy the fearsome giant."

And the knights thought, "This is all in a day's work." So they mounted their horses and they rode down the valley. Some way down the valley, the ground started to tremble and shake beneath them. As the giant reared up in front of them, they heard:

"*SWISH! SWASH! BANG! BOOOM!*
I AM YOUR NIGHTMARE!
I AM YOUR DOOM!"

Followed by *splat!* But they dodged the *splat!* and they looked up at the fearsome giant and they thought, "This is not in our job description." So they turned their horses and they rode back to the King and they said, "Your Highness, there are some things you just have to do yourself."

And the King knew it was his duty to get rid of the fearsome giant, but he wasn't that brave, but he did have a special friend, a mentor. Everyone should have one of these,

someone who you can go and share your problems with. For a problem shared is a problem halved. And the boy King's mentor was a woman called Sofia, the hen wife, the wise woman of the village. So he rode to Sofia's house and he knocked on the door.

A thin reedy voice said, "Come in!"

So he opened the door and he went inside. Sofia was sitting by the fire. On her lap was a large white hen. With one hand she stroked the hen and with the other hand she stroked her chin. The boy King stood in front of her, quaking with fear.

And she said, "What ever is the matter with you? Just sit down, count to ten. Calm yourself and tell me."

When he had calmed down, the boy King told Sofia that there was a fearsome giant that reared himself up in front of all of his subjects and they heard:

"*SWISH! SWASH! BANG! BOOOM!*
I AM YOUR NIGHTMARE!
I AM YOUR DOOM!"

Followed by *splat!* as it trod on them. And because he was the King, he had to do something to destroy the fearsome giant and he wasn't quite brave enough. He said, "That's right. What can I do?"

And Sofia said, "I will teach you a poem, and this poem will be useful to you.

We run from what we do not know,
And then it seems to grow and grow

And then it stands within our way
Until its name, we learn to say."

And the boy King thought, "That makes sense. Say it again."

"*We run from what we do not know,*
And then it seems to grow and grow
And then it stands within our way
Until its name, we learn to say."

And he thought, "That's right!" and he knew exactly what he had to do. So he thanked Sofia, and he walked out of the cottage and he mounted the horse, and he rode down the valley.

Some way down the valley, the ground started to tremble and shake beneath his feet, and the giant reared up in front of him, and he heard:

"*SWISH! SWASH! BANG! BOOOM!*
I AM YOUR NIGHTMARE!
I AM YOUR DOOM!"

Followed by *splat!* But he dodged the *splat!* and he looked up at the fearsome giant, and although his instinct was to run away, in his head, the voice of Sofia was whispering:

"*We run from what we do not know,*
And then it seems to grow and grow
And then it stands within our way
Until its name, we learn to say."

And he thought "That's right. I don't know the giant's name." So he dismounted, tied his horse to a boulder and, although his instinct was to run, he took one enormous step towards the giant. And as he did that, something very strange happened. The giant got a just tiny bit smaller. So he took a second step, and a third step. Every step towards the giant, the giant got smaller until he was no bigger than my thumb. And the boy King bent down and he picked up the tiny giant.

He stood him on the palm of his hand and he looked down at the giant and he said, “What is your name?”

And the giant looked up at him and said, “My name is Fear.”

Because sometimes, if we’ve got something we’re afraid of, we get so transfixed by the fear itself that it completely takes us over. And if we can identify that fear, and we might need the help of our mentor or special friend to do it, then we’re better able to deal with it. For that is the story of The Fearsome Giant.

Nyangara, the Fire Python

Retold by Jane Grell

Long, long ago, Nyangara the python lived in a cave at the top of a mountain. He was the only creature at that time to have fire, which he shared with no one. In fact, he used it to scare off the people who lived in the village below.

They steered well clear of him – that is, up until the time when their chief fell ill. Medicine men and women came from far and near with oils and ointments, potions and

poultices. They danced and sang, wove spells and chanted, but to no avail.

Then one day, in hobbled a wise old woman. She went past the group of elders gathered under a palm tree, straight into the chief's hut. Observing him closely, she pronounced, "Only Nyangara the fiery one can cure him now. Send for Nyangara."

The news spread like wildfire. Send for Nyangara? Who was there brave enough to go up the mountain and fetch Nyangara down?

The chief's eldest son volunteered. He was a hunter, brave, strong, famous throughout the region.

"I'll go," he boasted. "I'll hunt Nyangara down."

Up the mountain he went, approached the mouth of the cave and called out to the python.

"Nyangara, Nyangara, Nyangara!"

Angrily, the huge python uncurled his enormous body and slithered towards him. At the sight of Nyangara, the brave hunter turned and fled. With a huge gusty breath, the python sucked in all his clothes and ornaments. The hunter arrived in the village shaken, naked and ashamed.

The chief's second son stepped forward. He was a handsome athlete and dancer.

"I'll go," he said, flexing his biceps. But he ran off as soon as he heard Nyangara moving

in his cave. He too had his clothing sucked off his body and he arrived back in the village with blood-curdling accounts of his struggle with the fearsome python.

Naturally, the third son, a gifted woodcarver, felt obliged to try and save his father.

"I will entice Nyangara down," he said, softly. But of course, he suffered the same fate as his brothers.

One by one all the brave young men of the village tried, only to return humiliated. The villagers were in despair. Their chief would surely die. Then to everyone's amazement, up stood Amoafi, the chief's only daughter. Timidly, she stuttered,

"Pl … pl … please, may I go?"

This was greeted by peals of mocking laughter.

"You, a girl, who stutters too? You would go where all these brave young men have gone and failed!"

But as Amoafi persisted in her request, the elders gave in.

"Go then, daughter, and may the spirits of the ancestors protect you," they said.

Up and up the mountain she climbed. She got as near the mouth of the cave as she dared, took her courage in her hands and sang gently to the python.

> "*Nyangara, tie ha,*
> *Nyangara, tie ha.*" [1]

[1] Come here, Nyangara.

Three times she called to him in this way.

The sound of Nyangara's name echoed enchantingly over the valley, rousing him. What a surprise he had, to see the small creature who had woken him so pleasantly from his sleep. He was even more surprised that she hadn't run away as had all the others before her. The happy result was that Nyangara withheld his fiery breath.

Amoafi was thus able to explain her father's condition and especially what the old woman had said.

Nyangara was silent for what seemed like a hundred years, then he boomed, "I will come with you on one condition."

"What's that?" she asked.

"You will have to carry me down," replied the python.

"I will," agreed Amoafi, without thinking.

And so, ever so gently, the huge python wrapped himself around the girl's neck, around her shoulders and waist, way past her feet. Up until this day, no one knows just how she managed this heavy burden down the

mountainside right up to her father's bed.

Indeed, Nyangara was able to revive the chief. There was great feasting and rejoicing.

Before returning to his cave, Nyangara offered a gift to Amoafi as a reward for her bravery – a lighted torch.

"Take this torch. Use it wisely so no harm comes to you or your people. It holds much danger."

With that, Nyangara went up the mountain, back into his cave where, for all we know, he may still be asleep today.

Well, the torch did cause a lot of envy and bickering among the villages, but they've kept it burning from generation to generation.

Regrets

Retold by
Brian Patten

A group of men and women were on a journey to a new land. In order to get there, they had to pass through the Land of Darkness, where absolutely nothing could be seen.

They were stumbling through the Land of Darkness when under their feet, they felt small pebbles and heard a voice whisper,

> "*Whosoever takes some of these pebbles will regret it, and whosoever takes none will also regret it.*"

Some of the people thought, "If I'm going to regret taking the pebbles, I simply won't bother."

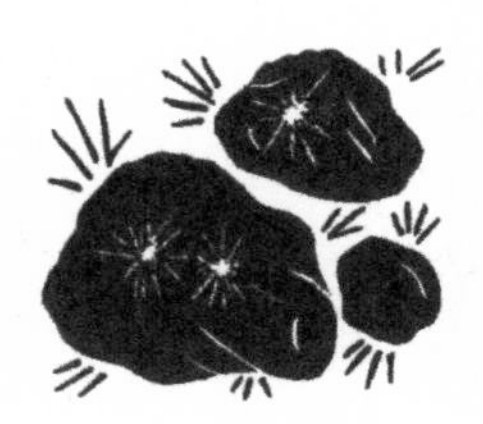

And others thought, "If I'm going to regret not taking any of the pebbles, then I might as well take at least one of them."

When the people came out into the light again, they discovered the pebbles were in fact lumps of pure gold. Those who had taken none regretted it. Those who had picked up only one lump of gold regretted they had not picked up more.

All carried their regrets to the grave.

The Impossible Escape

Retold by Pie Corbett

There was a man in prison who was famous for escaping – left all his captors gaping.

So they built him a room like a mummy's tomb in their finest jail and left him there to rot – not a jot of a chance to escape – no windows, and the doors held fast with the largest lock they had in stock!

All he had inside the room was a wooden table – and yet, acccording to the fable, ten minutes later he was free – so tell me, tell me, alligator, how was it done?

Answer:

Well, he rubbed his hands till they were sore. He took the saw and cut the table right in half. Two halves make a whole – so he climbed through the hole. Once outside, he cried till he was hoarse. He climbed on the horse and rode away...

The Widow's Daughters

Retold by
Patricia Leighton

Many years ago, in a land of fields, forests and flowing rivers, lived an old woman. Her husband had died when he was quite young and this left her with three small daughters to bring up all alone. They grew up beautiful, bright and happy, for their mother, although she was poor, worked long and hard to make sure that they had as much as she could give them.

The widow's beautiful daughters had no trouble finding three good husbands and, one by one, they left home. Now the widow was all alone, but she carried on working hard every day, for she still needed to grow food to feed herself, and to look after the hens who gave eggs which she could sell at the market.

Also, no matter how tired she was, the old woman always kept her small house spick and span.

And although she no longer had her daughters for company, and no close neighbours, she made friends with all the birds and creatures who came to her small garden. One particular favourite was the lively red squirrel which jumped down to chatter to her each morning when she put out scraps. The two became firm friends.

One day the old woman did not come out. The squirrel jumped in through an open window and found her huddled up in her bed, cold and shivering.

"You are ill," said the squirrel, quietly.

"I am dying," said the old widow. "Run and fetch my daughters so that I may see them one last time."

The squirrel raced off through the treetops until he came to the house of the widow's eldest daughter.

"Hurry, hurry!" he said. "Your mother is dying. You must come at once."

The eldest daughter, who had married a rich farmer, looked round her fine kitchen with all its pots and pans. She had such a lot to do.

"Of course I'll come ... as quickly as I can," she said, "but I must just finish cleaning my best china bowl and put it all away safely."

"Your bowl! Your bowl!" cried the squirrel angrily. And he looked at the eldest daughter long and hard. "Your time will come," he said, "then you will live for ever in your bowl."

The squirrel wasted no more time but hurried on to the house of the second daughter. She had married a weaver and together they had built up a very good little business.

"Your mother is dying and wants to see you," gasped the squirrel. "Come quickly, come quickly!"

"Oh, no!" cried the second daughter. She looked worried. "I'll come, of course, but I must just finish this piece of cloth. It's a very special piece for the Mayor and I dare not be late with it. I only have a little more to do. My husband and I will ride over as soon as we can, I promise."

The squirrel couldn't believe what he heard.

> *"Weave what? Weave cloth?" he said. And he looked at her long and hard. "Your time will come," he said, "and when it does, you will weave and weave, and never stop."*

Finally, the squirrel raced over to the youngest daughter, who lived in a cottage at the edge of a large wood. She had married the head woodsman on the Lord's estate and was mixing dough for bread, ready for when he came in from work. The squirrel rushed in.

"Hurry! Hurry!" he said. "Your mother is dying, poor thing. All she wants is to see her daughters before it's too late."

As soon as she heard the news, the youngest daughter dropped her spoon, grabbed

her shawl, and ran as fast as she could to her mother's house.

Her mother was still alive when she got there. She made up the fire and fed it with wood until the cottage was snug and warm once more. She held a cup to her mother's lips so that she could sip some water. The old woman was too weak for anything else but her face grew soft and she smiled gently as she looked at her daughter.

The youngest daughter stayed with her, stroking her hair and holding her hand, until the old woman gave a last sigh and died. The squirrel, who had been sitting on the pillow close to his friend, jumped into the young

woman's lap and reached up to wipe away the first tear that was running down her face.

> *"You are so sweet and kind," he said. "You will bring joy all your life wherever you go, and people will love you until the end of the world itself."*

So what became of the widow's three daughters when their times came?

The first daughter was counting her silver spoons when she felt her skin pull and puff and grow hard. Her head, her arms, her legs, began to wrinkle and shrink. She lived for evermore as a tortoise, trapped in her shell.

The second daughter was checking over a fine piece of cloth for any flaws when she felt her arms and legs grow long, and saw more arms and legs popping out of her side. She saw her belly turn black and shiny. Before she could scream, she had turned into a spider and knew that she would spin and weave, spin and weave, for ever more.

And the youngest daughter? Her time

came when she was sitting in the garden resting one bright sunny day, an old widow herself now. She felt herself become soft – she felt happy and light as air. She flapped her wings and flew off. She, her children and their children would bring sweetness to the world until the end of time.

She was a honeybee.

The Cobbler and the Dragon

Retold by Pie Corbett

In the days when trees could cry and cats could fly, there lived in Poland, underneath Wawel Hill, beside the Vistula River, a terrible dragon called Smok Wawelski.

First, Smok stole the cats and dogs. Next, he ate the sheep and cows. In the end, Smok paid his attention to grabbing young maidens!

Soon it was the turn of the King's daughter to be fed to the dragon. In desperation, he offered his daughter's hand in marriage to anyone who could rid the city of this terrible beast.

Princes came and princes went. Some ran as soon as they clapped sight on Smok. Others ventured under the hill and were never seen again. In the end, a cobbler called Krak came to the city.

"You'll never defeat the dragon," said the King, noticing that the cobbler had no sword.

"Do not worry," replied Krak. "I will give him a meal that he will not forget in a hurry!"

First, Krak took a leathery cow's skin.

Next, he stuffed it full of the hottest herbs and spices with a bag full of sulphur.

After that, he sewed the skin together to

make it look like a dead cow. He loaded his cart with that bulky bag, stuffed with such an explosive meal.

Early in the morning, he drove the cart by the river just as the mist was rising. There he unloaded his bulky gift and dragged it up to the very entrance of Smok's cave.

Inside it was dark. Krak peered in. He could just see the dragon, asleep on a pile of white bones. Its eye flickered open.

Without hesitating, Krak threw the mighty meal down into Smok's lair calling, "Dinner time, my beauty!"

The dragon ate it up in one huge *gulp!* At first, he felt a burning pain. Then his stomach roared like fire. Finally, his stomach roared in agony, so he flew to the River Vistula where he drank and he drank and he drank till the river was almost dry.

Of course, the more he drank, the more his stomach swelled. It swelled and it swelled and it swelled till in the end, it burst with a huge *bang!*

So it was that the cobbler married the

Princess and became King Krak. Why, he was so popular that they named the city after him – Krakow.

Ragamuffin and his Delicious Nail Soup

Retold by
Andrew Fusek Peters

Hungry Ragamuffin was tramping through the cold snow-bound night, when he saw a cottage whose windows glowed like gold from a fire in the hearth. His feet were frozen in his rickety boots and an icy wind blew through his torn and tattered coat. He marched up to the door and gave it a *rat-a-tat-tat*. Round the side of the door peered an old woman with a dried-up apple of a face.

"What do you want on this godforsaken night, beggarman?" she screeched.

"Only a simple bite to eat and a warm floor to lay this old and crooked body of mine!" he beseeched with a smile.

"I have not a smidgen of food, nor a drop of drink!" she grimaced. "So you'd best be gone from my door, beggarman!"

And with that she made to push it shut.

Quick as lightning, Ragamuffin put his foot in the way.

"Madam, if you have no food, you must be famished. Let me cook for you!" he smiled.

The old woman was taken aback. The tramp cook for her? Mind you, being a lazy sort, it would save her going to the trouble.

"Very well then, come in quick, but don't bring in the cold with you." She shuffled in and Ragamuffin rubbed his hands in glee at the warmth.

"Now my dear lady, fetch me a pot and some hot water." With curiosity and suspicion in her eyes, she did as she was told. As she brought in the pot, Ragamuffin reached into his greasy pockets and, with a flourish, pulled out an old rusty nail and plopped it in the water.

"Now tell me," asked the old woman, her eyes almost popping out, "what sort of meal is this?"

"Why, do you mean to tell me you've never heard of the famous Swedish dish, Nail Soup?"

"I can't say that I have, but it looks mighty interesting!" replied the stupid old woman.

Ragamuffin stirred the pot. "Now my poor nail has been on the boil all week, and he is indeed a bit weak. This soup needs thickening!" He turned to the old woman.

"Now, you would not happen to have a sprinkle of oatmeal to thicken it up, seeing as you have no food, that is?" smiled Ragamuffin with a twinkle in his eye.

"Oh, there might be a spot of that left

over," and she brought it straight in.

Ragamuffin stirred the pot. He bent over and sniffed. "Now that smells mighty fine, but this would be a feast fit for the gentry if we could add a little meat and the odd potato or two." He looked at the old woman and she, being very keen to impress the rich folk, vanished off to her larder.

"Now, Ragamuffin, I found us a nice bit of beef I had stashed away and some winter potatoes that I brought up from the cellar this very morning...". She paused. "Not that I have any food, you understand, just a few odd bits and bobs," she explained. In went the bits and bobs and soon a delicious aroma began to fill up the room.

Ragamuffin stirred the pot. "You know, I used to cook for the King himself..." said Ragamuffin as truthfully as he could, "and I have a feeling that if we could just add a handful of barley and a drop of milk, why this soup would soon be good enough to invite the King to partake!"

Such talk of royalty went to the woman's

head and she ran off to fetch the milk and the barley while thinking, "All this simply cooked with a nail!"

Ragamuffin stirred. He sniffed. He tasted and at last declared that the Nail Soup was ready.

"But really if the King and Queen were to drop by, they would want a sandwich to start, maybe a glass of good brandy, and the whole feast served on a decent white cloth!"

The old woman agreed heartily and went to do Ragamuffin's bidding.

And what a feast they had. As the old woman, full of grand thoughts, ate a grand meal, and after was so tired she was ready for even grander dreams. Ragamuffin himself, patted his round belly with pride and made to get up.

"Don't mind me, gracious lady, I am a mere tramp after all, and am happy now to go to sleep on your hard, cold, stone floor!" He grimaced as if his joints were aching and the old woman felt terribly guilty.

"That would never do for such a fine chef who has cooked for royalty no less. You shall have my bed for the night!" She made up the bed with crisp fresh sheets and a plumped-up pillow, heated water for the tramp to wash, and then let the not-so-raggedy Ragamuffin sleep in her room while she tossed and turned in a chair by the fire.

In the morning, after a fine and hearty breakfast, she turned to the wily tramp. "What can I offer, to buy that wonderful nail from you?" The old woman was desperate but greedy for a bargain.

Ragamuffin's eyes lit up. "Have you not a little gold for a poor old man?" The old woman went to find her hidden savings, and gave it him all. The nail was handed over and the old woman could not believe her luck. Her neighbours would be so impressed – or so she thought!

And with a ragbag of gold and a golden smile on his face, Ragamuffin, chef of the most Royal Nail Soup and the greatest liar that Sweden has ever seen, went on his merry way!

The Farmer's Fun-Loving Daughter

Retold by
Taffy Thomas

Somewhere in the heart of the countryside lived a farmer and his three children. He had two sons, who were intelligent, hard-working chaps. However, his daughter was a fun-loving partygoer.

The farmer was in the autumn of his years – the time was approaching when he would die. He knew he had to make a will to say which of his three children would inherit the farm. He went into town and called on the family lawyer.

He made a will stating that the day he was buried, each of his children was to be given one pound. They would have to use that pound to fill every room in the farmhouse from the ceiling to the floor. But the farmhouse was enormous and had one hundred and sixty-one rooms. This would be a test to see which of them should have the farm.

He was safe in the knowledge that he had made his will, and a couple of weeks later he took to his bed and died.

The day after his death, his three children took his coffin to the churchyard and buried him, full of years. After the ceremony, as the

family gathered in the farmhouse, the lawyer arrived to read them the will. All three were keen to know who would get the farm. The lawyer explained they were each to get one pound: they had to buy something to fill all one hundred and sixty-one rooms from the ceiling to the floor. Whoever could achieve this would inherit the farm.

The first of the intelligent, hard-working sons went out with his one pound and his horse and cart. He bought every second-hand feather mattress in the area. He returned to the farm and dragged the mattresses into the house. Taking his pocketknife, he slit the mattresses open and filled each of the one hundred and sixty-one rooms from the ceiling to the floor with … feathers.

The lawyer checked from room to room. It took so long to walk around one hundred and sixty-one rooms that by the time he came to the last one, the feathers had settled and there was a gap between the top of the feathers and the ceiling. The lawyer told the lad he liked the idea but that there was one room that wasn't quite filled, so he had failed in the task.

The second intelligent, hard-working son took a dustpan and brush and swept up all the feathers. He then went out with his pound and returned with a cardboard box. It was a box of candles. He stood a candle in each of the one hundred and sixty-one rooms. He had filled every room in the house with … light.

The lawyer checked from room to room. It took so long to walk around one hundred and sixty-one rooms that by the time he came

to the last one, the candle had gone out and it was in darkness. The lawyer told the lad that he liked the idea but that there was one room that wasn't quite filled, so he had failed in the task.

That left the fun-loving, party-going daughter. She went out with her one pound and returned with a small box containing a flute. She opened the door of every room in the house and sat cross-legged in the hall, playing a lively tune. All in the house started to smile and tap their feet. Some even started to dance.

She told the lawyer she had filled every room, not once, not twice, but three times. The lawyer was mystified and asked her to explain. She told him that, firstly, she had filled every room in the house with music. Secondly, everyone hearing it had started to smile, so she had filled every room with joy. And, thirdly, if you put music and joy together, she told him, you have life – so even at the time of her own father's death, she had filled every room in the house with life.

The lawyer – and even the brothers – were so impressed by her wisdom and spirit, that they agreed she should inherit the farm. Whether she gave up going to parties and became a hard-working farmer, or whether she carried on partying, or whether she did a bit of both, you would have to ask her … for she is the farmer's fun-loving daughter.

Bella and the Bear

Retold by Hugh Lupton

A story, a story!
Let it go, let it come!

Once upon a time there was a girl called Bella, and she was bold and brave and frightened of nobody. She was scared of nix-nought-nowt.

One fine day she pulled on her boots, buttoned her coat and tied her red headscarf under her chin. She picked up her basket, kissed her mother and father goodbye and went into the woods to pick berries.

All morning she filled her basket with bright red strawberries and dark blue bilberries and pale white cloudberries, until the air around her was sweet with the smell of them.

The air was so sweet with the berries she'd picked that a bear sniffed at the breeze and thought to himself, "*Aha!*"

A great brown bear sniffed at the sweet air and came lumbering through the trees towards her. When he saw Bella and her basket full of berries he slapped the pink pads of his paws together.

"*Aha*, my little one, you're the very thing I need. A pretty girl to be a servant."

And before Bella could say a word, the bear had snatched the basket from her hand, lifted her up and tucked her under his arm, and he was carrying her deeper into the dark woods than she'd ever been before.

Soon enough they came to a hut. The bear pushed open the door and dropped Bella on to the hard floor.

"Now then, my pretty one, you can set to work. There's plenty to be done."

Bella scrambled to her feet. There was plenty to be done all right. All afternoon she was cooking and cleaning and mending and making and baking. And all day the bear sat

and watched her, with the basket on his knees, lazily scooping Bella's berries into his mouth.

Bella made a big supper, and when the bear had eaten his fill, he stretched out on the floor with his back against the door and fell fast asleep.

She sat on a stool and stared at him.

She was bold and brave and frightened of nobody. She was scared of nix-nought-nowt.

And as she sat and stared she was thinking to herself, "How can I escape? How can I get safely home to my mother and father and away from this lazy, greedy, fat, brown furball of a bear?"

But there was no opening the door because the great brown weight of him was pressed against it.

Well, all the next day the brown bear was watching her with his bright, greedy little eyes. That evening, as the bear was gulping down his supper, Bella had an idea.

"Please, Mister Bear," she said, "tomorrow, will you take a present to my mother and father to show them that I'm alive and well?"

The bear grunted. "Maybe I will, maybe I won't."

"Please, Mister Bear, they will be wondering where I am and what's happened to me."

"Maybe I will, maybe I won't."

"Please, Mister Bear, if you take them a present I'll cook you a big supper when you get home."

"Maybe I will."

"A big supper with nuts and berries and honey and cakes and pastry and porridge."

The bear looked at Bella and licked his lips. "Maybe I will, my pretty one, for a supper like that."

"Mister Bear, I'll make them a present of pies, a basketful of cherry pies, but you mustn't touch them. You mustn't taste any of them. And when you get back home, I'll make you the biggest supper in the world."

The bear clapped the pink pads of his paws together. "I'll take them their present. For

a supper like that, I'll take them their present and I won't taste a crumb, I promise."

"Good," said Bella, "but be careful because I'll be watching you, and if you break your promise there will be no supper waiting for you when you get home."

"I promise, I promise." The bear lumbered across the room, he stretched out on the floor with his back to the door and fell fast asleep.

As soon as he was sleeping, Bella set to work. She set to making and baking cherry pies, lots and lots of them. When they were ready, she put four on the table for the bear's breakfast. Then she fetched a basket, a big one, climbed into it and covered herself with cherry pies. She lay curled up in the bottom of the basket with all the cherry pies on top of

her … and she waited.

When the bear woke up, he was hungry. He saw the four cherry pies on the table and gobbled them down. When he'd finished, he saw the basket on the floor. "There are all the cakes the little pretty one has made for her parents." He picked it up and set off through the trees towards the village. But the basket was heavy and soon his arm was aching.

"If I had a little rest," he said to himself, "and ate just one pie, no one would ever know the difference." He sat down on a tree stump.

But then he heard Bella's voice,"I'm watching. Don't break your promise!"

He looked over his shoulder."What sharp eyes the little pretty one has!"

The bear carried on walking.The basket seemed to get heavier and heavier. He carried it first on one arm, then on the other, then on his head.

"If I had a little rest now, she'd never see me, and just one little pie to give me strength for the journey." He sat down on a mossy tussock.

"I'm watching you. Don't break your promise!"

He looked over his shoulder. He couldn't see his hut at all.

"What sharp, sharp eyes the little pretty one has!"

He carried on walking. His arms were sore, his legs were sore, his back was sore, his tummy was rumbling with hunger. At last he saw the village ahead of him, the village where Bella's mother and father lived.

"If I had a little rest now it would give me strength to get home, and just one little pie for all my trouble."

He sat down on a rock, took a pie from the basket, and licked one sweet crumb from the edge of it with his red tongue.

"I'm on the roof. I'm watching you. You're breaking your promise."

The bear dropped the pie into the basket, leapt to his feet and ran into the village. "What sharp, sharp, sharp eyes the little pretty one

has!" He dropped the basket on the doorstep of her parents' house and ran back to the forest.

And when Bella's mother and father opened the door, the first thing they saw was the big basket of cherry pies, and then they saw Bella. She jumped out of the basket and into their arms.

"Bella, my darling, my sweetheart, where have you been?"

And Bella told her story from start to finish.

"But Bella, weren't you afraid?"

"I'm frightened of nobody. I'm scared of nix-nought-nowt."

And as for the bear, for that lazy, greedy, fat, brown, furball of a bear, when he got home he shouted, "Where's my supper, where are my nuts and berries and honey and cakes and pastry and porridge?"

But there was no answer.

"Where's the biggest supper in the world, my little pretty one?"

But there was no answer, and no supper, and why should there be? After all, he'd tasted a crumb and broken his promise.

And that is the end of that story.

Cinderella

Retold by Pie Corbett

Once there was a young girl and her mother died, so she was buried beside the river. When winter came, the snow spread a white sheet over the grave. When in spring the sun drew it off again, her father had taken another wife.

The woman brought her two daughters to live in the house. Though they were beautiful, their hearts were ugly and harder than stone.

"If you want bread, you must earn it," snapped the sisters at the young girl.

They took away her clothes so she had to wear an old grey gown and wooden shoes. They made her carry the water, light the fires, cook and scrub. Day after day they fed her

scraps till in the end she became so thin that her ribs jutted out and her arms were thinner than chicken bones. And late in the evening, the only place to sleep was by the fireside in the warm ashes. Because she was so dusty and dirty, they called her Cinderella.

Now one day her father went to the fair.

He brought both girls beautiful dresses, pearls and jewels, but he forgot to buy Cinderella anything. So on the way home, he

pulled a branch from a tree that had a few white blossoms upon it, for it reminded him of his first wife.

So Cinderella went down to the river and she planted that branch on her mother's grave. She sat there staring at the few ragged blossoms and cried so much that her tears moistened the soil.

Later that day, she came back to the grave and instead of a branch, there was a small bush, a beautiful bush with white blossom that smelt so sweet. Sitting on the bush was a small white bird. How sweetly it sang! And under the bush was a small cloth and on the cloth some food – bread and cheese and an apple. So it was every day, three times a day, and whatever she needed, the bird sang and it appeared under the bush.

Now the King held a festival for three whole days to which all the young girls were invited so that the Prince might choose a bride. The girls ordered Cinderella, saying, "Comb our hair, buckle our shoes, tighten this dress!" Even though she pleaded to join them,

her stepmother would not allow it. "We would be ashamed of you!" she snarled.

And so Cinderella went down to the river and kneeled by her mother's grave, weeping so bitterly. Then she sang the words of a lullaby that her mother had sung to her as a child, words she had never quite understood,

> "*Shiver and quiver, little tree,*
> *Silver and gold throw on to me.*"

And when she opened her eyes, there it was under the bush – a gold and silver dress and slippers embroidered with silk and silver.

So she went to the ball and the Prince would dance with no one else. He was swept away in the flight of the dance and the beauty of that girl. But later that night she escaped from the Prince and hid in the pigeon cote, ashamed of her state.

Two nights this happened, but on the third the Prince smeared the palace steps with cobbler's wax, so her left slipper remained sticking there, dainty and golden.

The Prince set out the next day to visit house after house saying, "No one shall be my wife but she whose foot fits this slipper."

Cinderella's two stepsisters were delighted, for they had dainty feet. First, the eldest tried it on. But it would not fit, so she squeezed it tight till in the end it was on. But as she rode past the mother's grave, the white bird sang,

"*Turn and look, turn and look,*
There's blood in the shoe.
The true bride still awaits for you."

Sure enough, blood seeped from the slipper where her foot was squeezed too tight.

Next, the second girl tried it on. But it would not fit, so she squeezed it tight till in the end it was on. But as she rode past the mother's grave, the white bird sang,

"Turn and look, turn and look,
There's blood in the shoe.
The true bride still awaits for you."

Sure enough, blood seeped from the slipper where her foot was squeezed too tight.

"Is there not another daughter?" asked the Prince.

"No – only the kitchen girl my first wife left behind," replied the father.

"No, no – she is too dirty; she must never be seen," replied the stepmother.

Then the Prince sent for Cinderella and the slipper fitted like a glove. As the Prince and Cinderella rode past the tree, two white birds flew down and they perched on her shoulders, one on each. And they stayed there till she reached the palace.

The two sisters and the stepmother ranted and raved, but it was to no avail.

And the father – who was not a father – well, I'll leave his end to you.

"*Be it grim or be it kind –*
Look in your heart,
To see what you find."

About the authors

Xanthe Gresham

Xanthe Gresham (pronounced "Zanthee") is a full-time storyteller. She began storytelling in 1995 and is popular with both adults and children. She has worked in the UK, Ireland, France, New Zealand, Slovenia, Holland and Switzerland. She will tell her stories almost anywhere. For example, she has had audiences in theatres, schools, museums, galleries, festivals, hospitals, community spaces, roundhouses, barges, boats, gardens, parks, woodlands and in waiting rooms!

Xanthe has worked extensively for the British Museum. She works as a storyteller for Holland Park and the Chelsea Physic Garden and is a Lecturer in Storytelling and Drama at the University of East London.

Taffy Thomas

Taffy Thomas is a leading and experienced storyteller. In the past he trained as a Literature and Drama teacher and then taught for several years. He then founded the travelling theatre and arts companies Magic Lantern, and Charivari, and then returned to concentrate on storytelling.

Taffy has a repertoire of more than 300 stories, collected mainly from oral sources. Taffy often wears his famous Tale Coat when telling stories – a beautiful embroidered coat which displays intricate images from many of the stories Taffy loves to tell.

Taffy has appeared at arts festivals in the USA and in Norway. In 2001 he performed for the Blue Peter Prom at the Royal Albert Hall; and in 2006 was storyteller in residence at the National Centre for Storytelling in Tennessee. Taffy is currently the artistic director of Tales in Trust, the Northern Centre for Storytelling, in the Lake District. In the 2001, he was awarded an MBE for services to storytelling and charity. He tours nationally and internationally, working both in entertainment and education, and is also a patron of the Society for Storytelling.

Pie Corbett

Pie Corbett is an extremely well known and prominent figure in the field of education. He has worked as a primary teacher and headteacher and has also worked as an English inspector in Gloucestershire.

He edits, compiles and writes poetry books for children. He also writes resource books for teachers. He has published over 200 books. He is a selector for the 'Children's Poetry Bookshelf' and also wrote poetry objectives for the National Literacy Strategy.

In addition to his writing, Pie also runs writing workshops, runs In-service training, performs poetry and takes part in storytelling events all over the country. He has also appeared at numerous literary festivals such as those at Cheltenham, Edinburgh and Wiltshire. He is currently working with the Story Museum in Oxford as co-director of their educational outreach programme.

Jane Grell

Jane Grell was born and grew up on the island of Dominica. She has been running storytelling workshops for children and adults since 1986. Now living in London, she has taken her stories to audiences around the UK. She draws heavily though not exclusively on her African-Caribbean heritage. Her storytelling thus consists of rhythm games, songs, poems, proverbs, riddles and stories.

Jane's stories have been published in various anthologies. She has worked as a writer/presenter on BBC School Radio and is a frequent contributor to Scholastic's *Literacy Time* and *Child Education*.

Hugh Lupton

Hugh Lupton became a professional storyteller in 1981. In 1985 he formed the Company of Storytellers and for twelve years the company toured Britain. Hugh has toured Africa and South America for the British Council and regularly performs in Europe and the USA. He has published several collections of folk tales.

Helen East

Helen East was born in Colombo but settled in London in 1979, where she started working as a storyteller. She has directed several major regional arts and storytelling projects. Since 2002 Helen has regularly led storywalks in Shropshire and the borders. She has also led storywalks in Kew Gardens, London. She has toured South America, telling stories in primary and secondary schools.

Andrew Fusek Peters

Andrew Fusek Peters began storytelling in the 1980s. His stories came from his own Czech background, Aboriginal culture and the revived oral tradition in the UK. He has written and edited over 60 books for young people. His storybooks and novels include *The Barefoot Book of Strange and Spooky Stories, Roar! Bull! Roar!, Falcon's Fury* as well as the exciting thriller series *Skateboard Detectives*.

Daniel Morden

Daniel Morden is one of the UK's most popular storytellers. He regularly appears at The National Theatre and The Barbican Centre. He has travelled the world, from the Arctic to the Pacific to the Caribbean. His recent book *Dark Tales from the Woods* won the Welsh Books Council Tir Na Nog prize.

Patricia Leighton

Patricia Leighton principally writes children's poetry. She has also done work for the 'poetryclass' scheme run by the Poetry Society which provides guidelines and contacts for the use of poetry in schools. She has also written short stories and resource materials for the primary age range.

Brian Patten

Brian Patten is one of the most accessible and popular poets working today. He made his name in the 60s in the

Liverpool trio with Adrian Henri and Roger McGough and has been writing and performing poetry ever since. Brian writes and edits poetry for both adults and children, he is widely published and his poems have been translated into many languages.